SANDY
AND
WAYNE

by

STEVE YATES

Southern Hollow Press

SOUTHERN HOLLOW PRESS
Flowood
fictionandhistory.wordpress.com

Originally published in 2015 by
Dock Street Press, Seattle

Copyright © 2015 Steve Yates, renewed 2020

All rights reserved, including right of reproduction
in whole or part of any form.

This is a work of fiction. Names, characters, places, and incidents either
are the product of the author's imagination or are used fictitiously.
Any resemblance to actual persons, living or dead, events, or locales
is entirely coincidental.

ISBN: 978-1-0879-1862-4
EBOOK AVAILABLE

Front cover photograph courtesy Curtis Photography LLC,
www.curtisphotographyllc.com
from The Wild Horses of Shannon County

This book is for Jane & Randolph.

SANDY
AND
WAYNE

There is nothing like walking behind a thoroughbred filly on a freezing morning, watching that bounding step, those jouncing back pasterns—two pinion-feather-pogo springs, that roll of the big, eager eyes, that steaming breath with every nod of the head. Nothing like it to make a woman wonder, Why? Why these hills, these stars, that fog, these acres, this ready animal, why us, alone? It would make some fine kind of country song, Sandy Coker reflected, key of G, like her late father used to play, with his extra flourish, that ring finger on the B string, three frets up, so that the already pretty chord rang like a bell on a bald.

She led her horses to pasture, lingering with Trick of Light, her filly. The animal was strengthening. Very soon she would be in heat. With a hope she distrusted but enjoyed just the same, Sandy ran through her plan of attack to market the filly's receptive season. Sandy would call her cousin, the vet to half a dozen stables in Hot Springs, and her two friends who were breeders. This might be the year some hungry owner would partner with Sandy for the chance at a foal that could claim Phone Trick in its bloodline. Her other horses, wonderful for riding but no thoroughbreds, felt Trick of Light was an imperious and pampered alien. In the fog coming up from White River, the other horses huddled in contented, separate company. When she left, Sandy could feel Trick gazing after her all the way up the hill to the trailer.

The Early Ag report on television began talking about a comet that was to be far more spectacular than Halley's Comet. Sandy slowly turned her coffee mug against the countertop. Something plunked on the roof of her double-wide, and the skitter of a squirrel's running made the trailer seem like an empty tube. She turned off the coffee, disgusted with herself that she was yet again throwing away half a pot. The Ag reporter was excitedly pointing out where to look for this comet, and Sandy longed for her father to be there watching this with her. She was thirty-seven now and alone still after a year without him. He could tell her if this really was a comet worth losing sleep to see. When she turned the knob to shut off his black-and-white television, the trailer took on that extra stillness just before sunrise. She recalled an old pair of his work gloves she had pitched yesterday, the fingers full of hardened clay. Holding her cup against her chest, Sandy searched the silence until she could hear, not far away, the moan of big rigs on blacktop.

When she ground the battered, white carryall to a halt, she relished the dust rolling over the hood, the spattering lime thrown forward. Her rowdy entrance into the gravel lot of the Maurer Construction headquarters on Highway Job AR4005 stirred nothing in the contractor's green trailer. Even when she slammed the carryall door, the blinds on the trailer didn't rise, the front door didn't pop open. The air conditioner rattled, but everything else was silent.

This was a moment she looked forward to, anticipating the shock and eventual smugness when a salty bunch of foremen first faced the lead inspector of the Arkansas Highway and Transportation

Department and found her to be a sun-hardened, blond, blue-eyed gal no bigger than a jockey.

Today's meeting bore more than the usual potential for sweet fracas—Maurer was a hotshot company down from Missouri, the first northern bunch in a long while to win a contract in the Arkansas Ozarks. Maurer took over AR4005 when the original contractor went bankrupt. Among contractors rumor circulated it was Sandy and her rigid standards and confrontational tendencies that sank the initial bidder. One slip of a gal broke a great big company. This new outfit, Maurer, had a reputation that carried smoke and sulfur as well. Talks with the sole cement vendor in Northwest Arkansas ended in a fistfight and jail time for the Maurer negotiator. Bets were rumored all around the office. How long until a dustup forced Sandy Coker to endure chair duty with the chief engineer in Springdale?

She took the steps and pulled open the door, expecting to surprise a covey of randy men. Instead just one lean fellow hunched in a metal chair.

When he turned to see who had intruded on him, she saw his eyes so silver-blue they could have been circles of mercury. He did not rise, did not even wave at her to take a seat. In one hand he gripped the microphone to a radio set. In the other hand he pinched a cigarette, holding it so lightly, Sandy thought he might flick it away any second.

A swarm of nonsense buzzed from the radio.

The man smiled at the set. Watching the light blue cast of his eyes, Sandy sensed a joy in him, a delight in whatever he was doing. Pinpricks of embarrassment crossed her hairline. To stave off this strange feeling, she lit a Marlboro and waited.

"It's a permit you have to get, 01, over," the man said. Tubes in the back of the radio glowed a grungy orange when he spoke. "Otherwise we'll have to wait on another thirty-day window, over." His accent was clearly country, but nothing like Sandy's. He sounded like people she knew from Kansas City.

The radio crackled. "Do it in my sleep," the

man answered. "4005 out."

When he finished he pushed the mic back on the clean desk and faced her. The whole of the trailer, its linoleum and countertops, metal file cabinets, its plans rolled neatly on heavy wooden dowels, everything was more spic and span than any headquarters she could recall. But she chalked this up to Maurer just beginning on AR4005.

"What's this you do in your sleep?" Sandy asked him.

He grinned more broadly, and she noted that his straight teeth were not too yellow. His hair was peppered gray, but thick and wavy. He seemed mischievous and appealing to her, more than was safe for him to be.

"Better not say." He flicked the cigarette on the linoleum and pressed it out quickly and efficiently with the heel of his work boot. "So you must be the Arkansas Highway Department's idea of a lead inspector?"

Here was the attitude she expected. "Idea? I'm the fact, buster."

He didn't rise but stuck out his hand. "I'm Wayne."

"Sandy," she said, squeezing his hand lightly. With men she didn't play the bullshit of firm grips. And as it often did with others, this disarmed him when he found his large, rough hand daintily squeezed by one every bit as hardened as his own, yet delicate and almost out of place in its gentleness. "How about I introduce you to a 1.3-million-dollar bungle?"

"Sugar, we just met!"

She smiled but held back a witty rejoinder that came to mind—what she was about to show him would ruin his week. "You like to have fun, don't you, Wayne?"

His smile faded, and he watched her with a calm that was starting to rankle her.

She edged right up to his face until, despite her own cigarette, she could smell the mentholated smoke clinging to his hair. "If you call me anything but Sandy in front of the rest of your crew or anyone on my team, you are going to long for a Missouri lawyer, and Maurer's going to want to say goodbye to you and all Arkansas."

He frowned and raised his eyebrows. "So you're the gal that ran that other outfit into arrears." Then his smile slowly returned. "Show me what's the big trouble."

In his small, hunter green Ford, just like the ones she had seen Maurer surveyors driving, he followed her across the cut, bouncing, careening, and winding over huge drifts of dirt as red as the surface of Mars. Here the initial stages of excavation were done—clearing and grubbing, blasting, then the disastrous earthwork that submerged Maurer's predecessor. The failed company left a five-mile-long scar in the earth. Steep exposed limestone bluffs topped with oaks and hickory set off a mess of red clay down in the basin. She and Wayne pitched and rocked among tremendous boulders and the abandoned, battered equipment that creditors could not repossess: the blades of great dozers, the rusting derrick to a crane, a massive diesel engine with a cracked block, fuel tanks, machine shacks, a hard hat bearing the vanquished company's blue symbol and some worker's stenciled name, sun scorched and now illegible. There was so much failure seeded here it made Sandy shiver passing the bad luck of each ruin. Soon they hit a frontage road with asphalt black and perfect, not even a line striped on it yet save the red smears left by their tires.

She stopped where the frontage road finished in a cul-de-sac. When Wayne stepped from his truck his forehead wrinkled, but he kept smiling. At the end of the cul-de-sac and its brand-new asphalt was an astonishing drop-off. The end of the frontage road essentially created a ramp into the blue yonder.

Wayne stood on the curb looking out over a forested holler and at least a two-story plunge. It bothered Sandy that she liked the jeans he was wearing and the way they molded to his long legs and muscular behind when he arched his back and stretched his arms out, yawning. "Hell of a view," he said.

She scowled. "Help me with something, Wayne. What will happen when some teenager three sheets to the wind comes hauling ass down through here at midnight and doesn't notice that this pretty, new road ends all of a sudden in wide open sky?"

Wayne nodded. "Guard rail and warning signs will have to be put up." He surveyed the screwup a bit longer. To the trained eye it was clear that the previous contractor had built up this dirt, and a lot of it, to achieve such an elevation. Then they had paved it over and made their folly permanent. "Listen, doesn't Arkansas have any control over who's allowed to bid down here?"

Sandy snorted. "Of course."

"Well, what in the world happened? I mean, you would have to work overtime at stupid to achieve some of the nonsense this last bunch stuck you with."

So he was capable of rancor and disgust. She dared approaching him and patting his arm. "There, there. Those bad boys left you a mess."

Wayne's face drew a flat line of stillness and distance so rapidly it startled her. "You know, Sandy, the Missouri Highway Commission blackballed those clowns three years before you all ever let the bid on this. Blackballed. Permanent." He felt his shirt pocket for his cigarettes. "All your commissioners had to do was pick up a phone and ask."

You Yankee asshole, she thought, glad she was not finished vexing him. "Well, get a load of this, Mr. Wisdom," she said, waving him over. She led him to a break where the curb and gutter dove into a driveway that was hidden by the treacherously elevated frontage road. The gravel drive had more pitch than most rooftops. Way down at the bottom was an A-frame house. Laundry flapped, and a big, gray husky tied to the clothesline watched them with its pink tongue lolling.

Wayne removed his green Maurer ball cap and stared at the drive for a long while. "Crap," he said finally. "Crap."

"I'd like you to come meet the momma who's

going to have to drive up this ski slope in rain and snow and ice." She turned sideways to let her work boots skid down the grade, it was that steep. Together they passed the husky dog. Both she and Wayne paused. What had appeared to be a sled dog turned out to be solid gray with yellow eyes. It watched them with a wariness unlike any dog Sandy knew. The rope that tied it to the clothesline looked like it had been salvaged from a lake, it was so gray and crusty.

"Now, Mrs. Yarberry is one of us," Sandy said. "Her husband's down near Fort Smith, building that tunnel. Only home on weekends."

Wayne nodded. "That's hard enough on her," he said, still watching the dog.

On the porch of the A-frame a thin, pale woman with black rings under her eyes and straight, dark, greasy hair stared out at a toddler. The youngster darted toward Sandy and Wayne, and Sandy stopped in surprise. The little one didn't toddle or wobble, but zipped forward, then dodged and circled them on legs that seemed far too balanced and sure for her age. When Wayne halted dramatically and made a face, the youngster laughed and ran to her mom. Her curly, red hair bounced behind her.

"Mrs. Yarberry, this is Wayne and he's from Mizz Ooo Raw," Sandy said. She wanted to be vicious. Look what a fix this poor mother was left in! "He works for that contractor up the hill. Them dark green trucks you been seeing."

Wayne still had his hat off, and he appeared silly to Sandy, wadding that hat against his belt buckle, looking penitent. "Ma'am, are you having trouble getting up that drive?"

"Goddamn right I am." The exhausted mother kept her black-rimmed eyes on the toddler, who hustled over to Sandy and held up some blades of plantain.

"O dour," said the child. "Du jour." Unlike the mother, she had an elfish face, narrow chin, round cheeks. "Dan jour." She pressed the plantain leaves in Sandy's palm.

The tired mother shook her head. "Don't you

all think by two she should be talking English? But, I swear to God, this funny French shit is all that comes out of her mouth."

Sandy prompted Mrs. Yarberry to talk about her husband and the hard fact of him being gone so often. The mother got into quite a jag, and it was clear she missed having someone to talk to. When she paused, Wayne began to propose some ideas about how Maurer could bring the driveway around the house and lessen the incline, even pave it, all for free. He stooped sometimes talking with her, as if he were so tall he had to bring the words down to her to be heard.

The tyke pulled Sandy toward the clothesline and the strange, gray dog, which watched the child with an interest that began to bother Sandy. The dog was too alert, and reminded her of a coyote in the way its eyes shifted but its head remained still.

"Oh, she loves that doggy, Siska," the mother said. "Say 'doggy,' sweetie. Just one time say something English." The child waved at the dog. "Ninety-eight percent wolf that one. My husband drove all the way to Idaho to pick that wolf-dog out himself."

Wayne looked at Sandy.

She was about to go into an explanation of the mother's rights, the redresses the poor woman could demand of Maurer, when the child jerked on both of Sandy's hands, making her arms go stiff. Sandy tried to straighten up, but the child gripped her hands more firmly and in one deft move she leapt, planted her bare feet on Sandy's shins, up on her thighs, still running, then flipped herself ass end over and landed on both feet facing the wolf, still holding on to Sandy's fingertips with her arms thrown back.

"Oh my," Sandy exclaimed. Wayne's eyes were wide.

"Sweetie, I told you that scares people," the mother griped. She reached out, but the laughing girl released Sandy and ran away. When the wolf lunged, the rope gagged it and whirled it off its feet.

Sandy caught a glance from Wayne that told

her she was not alone in her unease. Wayne took over the talking and soon got the Mrs. Yarberry to agree to let him bring a crew down and swing the driveway to a part of the frontage road that would make it less troublesome.

Sandy gave the young mother her state mobile phone number and told her to call if Maurer was too slow, or if she needed anything with her husband away.

Walking back up the driveway with the wolf watching them, Sandy felt an unfamiliar closeness with this contractor, as if somehow she and Wayne were both in danger.

"Ninety-eight percent wolf," Wayne said under his breath.

Sandy found herself frowning. She thought of the girl's French, her gymnastics, and her daddy so far away blasting a tunnel through the Boston Mountains for the highway. Highway work pulled people apart, left wives, lovers, families alone. It was often dangerous for the workers and sometimes even for the inspectors. She had walked pigeon-toed along many a narrow, knobby bridge girder, deadly heights above valleys, to turn in the wind and face the faraway theodolite, safe on an embankment. She glanced at Wayne's hands and saw no ring. Like her, he was probably alone. "You better take good care of that poor lady."

Wayne nodded.

By the sheer volume of what was moved, what was excavated and shaped on the earth, no item on an interstate job paid more than dirt. And no operation could slowly and stealthily erode and eventually consume a construction company's finances like earthmoving if it were mismanaged. Next to the estimator—an engineering and finance wizard—the dirt foreman, Wayne, that estimator's proxy on the ground, was the most crucial hire in a workforce. When Sandy watched Wayne among his fellow foremen, she saw the deference they paid him. He was not a talker in company, joked only when he had you one-on-one. But when he spoke, his mates fell silent and listened closely.

The day Maurer's heavy equipment was to arrive on the job, Wayne marshaled a row of three tanker trucks full of diesel. On the radio, on television, in the papers came the announcement that Arkansas Highway 468 would be closed that morning. Permits were in order, and before dawn, flashing barriers went up, highway patrol posted officers, and flaggers mustered.

Sandy lit a cigarette and walked over to Wayne's pickup. Wayne was leaning against the open door, the CB mic in his hand.

He winked at her. "You know, in Missouri there'd be no way in the world you could get an inspector out at this hour."

"Glad to know we're doing something right down here."

He smiled. "Didn't say it was right."

After some chatter crackled up from his CB, Wayne leaned in the truck window and blew the horn three times.

Back in the darkness, miners' lights snapped on atop hardhats. Flashlights lit and threw frantic bolts. From tents, pickups, and carryalls, dark figures emerged and stretched. Far off against the black, ragged tree line, the flash of an arc welder sparked. On each of the fuel trucks, fog lights glowed, and men in green jumpers stood ready. Sandy marveled at this for a moment—Maurer had brought in far more forces over the last week than any company she had inspected. With a shudder she recalled the haphazard way the previous, failed company had mustered heavy equipment onto the job, how she would catch them driving some gargantuan scraper across a county road with no permit, obliterating shoulders and tearing the roadbed into chunks.

"Cold?" Wayne handed her a Styrofoam cup of coffee.

Sandy took the cup and thanked him.

Very soon Peterbilts with long trailers arrived, twelve of them, and on each trailer rode a yellow Caterpillar earthmover dismantled so that its cab, engine, and yoke tilted on one end of the trailer. The scraper and maw rested on the back. The machines looked like deep-bellied, yellow tiger beetles with their heads split off.

The Peterbilts lined up in pairs. On the trailers of the lead pair, men scrambled. They rattled chains loose and quickly unlimbered iron ramps down into the dewy, red soil. With the help of a track hoe that had an iron hook on its bucket, men with acetylene torches and tremendous wrenches set to work fastening the giant bellies of each earthmover to the cabs and engines.

In the commotion, Wayne left her side and took a seat on the cab of the first Caterpillar assembled. With a grunt and a long squirt of black smoke from its stack, it rumbled awake. Wayne backed the yellow monster down the two ramps as the Peterbilt edged forward. With another growl and shot of black smoke, the Caterpillar surged to the side then lurched to a stop beside the fuel tanker. There Wayne cut the engine. Gasmen in green jumpers clambered up on the earthmover with fuel lines cradled in their arms.

Wayne hopped down and shouted at the next

crew waiting in line. The Peterbilt he had unburdened smoothly pulled away just as another gurgled into its place.

Wayne walked back to her, wiping his hands and forearms on a cloth black with grime. He tossed it down at his feet. Mechanics bearing grease guns tended the joints and bearings of the Caterpillar as it fueled. Behind them, the dawn sent a silver curtain across the east.

She appreciated this outfit's agility. From wherever they had bought or leased these scrapers, Maurer hauled not even a single extra ounce of fuel, not a spurt of excess grease. Even some of the massive cotter pins they brought from stores on site. Each scraper arrived, she figured, with just enough fuel to start it, back it off the semi, and land it empty next to the fuel tanker.

"Well, lead inspector?" he asked, lighting a Salem. The flames threw an orange light on his face. The solid chin, the sharp nose, the clean-shaven jaw irked her. With a country girl's hard-bitten sense, she was suspicious of good-looking men from more sophisticated parts of the Ozarks.

"Oh, I seen that other bunch arrive with just as much flare," she lied.

"But did you yourself come to see them marshal up?" Wayne asked. "Personally?"

It occurred to her that Wayne had access to the Daily Diary of AR 4005, the running record she was required to keep of everyday happenings along the jobsite. Unlike most other contractors she knew, he might be one to read it. After what she had seen this morning, she was sure he knew the answer to his own question. He was a step ahead of her.

"It's what you do after you unload that matters," she said.

Cigarette glowing, he turned to face the operation as she was seeing it and stood uncomfortably close, his warm hip and hard belt catching her just below her ribs.

Up above in the sky, now turned navy blue, a star with a long silver tail hung. The tail ran askew in a direction the mind couldn't put right, especially when the streak didn't vanish but seemed to have skidded to a stop. It had to be that comet, Hale-Bopp, which she had heard so much about on the Early Ag report.

"I thought cosmic events were supposed to make you feel like a tiny dot in a vast universe," said Wayne.

Freshly full of diesel, the next scraper roared, then advanced toward them. When its driver wove side-to-side, swung the scraper's maw up and down to test the hydraulics, the huge yellow earthmover seemed to wag and dart, its head independent of a swinging tail and torso. They reminded Sandy of mink she had seen chasing and fighting on White River when she was a young girl, only these were animals of metal, impossibly large, fiercely unnatural, save for the speck of a driver hovering in the cab far above the dirt.

"You feeling tiny, Wayne?"

He blew a long breath of smoke into the air, watching the scraper twist and rumble down the red scar of earth. "Goliath couldn't touch a hair on my head."

Back at the Springdale office filing paperwork at 5 p.m., Sandy declared this to be a star-crossed night. She and Phyllis, the office manager, met at The Limelight Lounge near their homes in Greenland to shoot pool and share a couple pitchers.

Phyllis left the bar early. Sandy was finishing a game when Wayne walked into The Limelight and arranged four quarters on her table. He didn't say a word to her or her opponent. Maybe his height caused this, but Wayne made quite a show picking out a cue, holding each tip to his eye and staring down the cue to its base to judge if the stick were true or warped.

"Wayne, I got a level in the truck if you need to be precise." Leaning on her cue, she felt jaunty, even playful. Though Maurer had rented out all the rooms in a decaying motor lodge not far down the road, Wayne was in her territory. "How'd you find this place, Wayne?" She glanced at her opponent who was agonizing over a bank shot.

"Is there another bar in Greenland, Arkansas, with more than one pool table?" He was right—if he enjoyed pool he would have found The Limelight.

When the barkeep brought her and Wayne bottles of Busch and indicated that it was on Wayne's tab, the feeling of sport evaporated. Those blue eyes, that clean, wavy hair just starting to gray, the strong jaw, the overconfident smile—in her lifetime she had seen a lot of mighty good-looking men who were entirely full of shit.

She considered throwing the game so that she didn't have to play Wayne. But then with a touch of beery rationale she decided if she did beat her opponent, then she would put it in the hands of fate, whatever happened, even if she and Wayne woke up from a blind drunk the next afternoon in some ticket line at the Memphis airport headed for Vegas. She ran her last four balls and sank the eight, nearly scratching, the cue ball hanging on the pocket's edge.

As Wayne dropped his quarters and began placing the balls in the rack, she finished the Busch. Just as she suspected he would, the barkeep came around with another, set it beside her and withdrew. Wayne did not rack quickly and made no show of experience. He slipped each ball in the plastic triangle after scrutinizing the scarred surfaces. Finally bending to the rack, he paused, then fell to picking at the felt.

"There have been children conceived on this table, Wayne. There's no making it pretty."

He set the rack. "What would that do to a person's lifeline, I wonder?" He grinned at her with eyes as bright as cheap, blue topaz in that dark bar. "Can you imagine telling your kids: 'Well, daughter, I was likely the product of a screw on a pool table in The Limelight Lounge, Greenland, Arkansas. Felt and slate I'm mighty partial to."

On the break she pocketed a stripe and a solid, one more portent that this was a crossroads. "Is that the way people get a destiny, Wayne?"

She sank another solid.

"Yeah, sure," Wayne said. "Lonely people making forlorn babies."

Loneliness was not a subject she wanted explored. A bumper proved harder than she called it and pocked her object ball back out into the green, but left the cue ball stuck against the opposite rail. "Too much talk," she said.

Wayne nodded. He played in that infuriating style she had seen among kids who grew up in pool halls and bar rooms, shooting one-handed, taking no time whatsoever to align shots or judge distances. He came at the table from rash angles, poking and stabbing in jolts that made her fearful he would rip the felt and be thrown out of the bar for good. But what resulted was breathtaking.

Shots that made no apparent sense fell.

At first his style distracted her, but she took his measure and evened the game. Very soon the two of them fell into the pleasurable trance of balls tocking, enjoying the deep thrum after they dropped to gurgle along the unseen, mysterious chutes down inside the table. The country music, the smoke and loud chatter of the bar vanished. They shot in silence, playing quickly and decisively. She felt a contagious grace growing between them as each shot improved on the previous, each leave opened possibilities. When Wayne scratched on the eight, it was a letdown.

"One more?" Wayne asked.

She shook her head. "I got horses to feed."

Wayne's eyes widened. "What I wouldn't do to see a horse. That's something I hate about this job. A horse could never depend on me, so I can't keep one back home. And I got to go all the way to Sallisaw to see one."

She wrinkled her nose. "Those are hardly what I'd call real horses."

"Oh?"

"I got me a filly out of Phone Trick waiting on me."

Wayne finished his beer. "Well, let's not keep her waiting."

"Not so fast," she said. "I'm not giving any free tours at Coker Farm this season. If you want to see horses, you're going to have to shovel some shit, mister."

"Won't be my first time, I assure you," he said.

He settled the tab and she told him to follow her. They left down a back road from The Limelight—she didn't want to court the chance that anyone in Greenland might see her on the main drag, leaving a beer joint, being followed by a contractor, even though Wayne was driving his own car and not a Maurer truck. He drove a Camaro, a 1980s model, which had been primered gray and sanded. But here he was scratching and banging it along dirt and gravel roads every evening in Arkansas. When they stopped on the hill in the gravel driveway to her farm, she couldn't help but notice how the white lime of the drive had dinged and frosted the Camaro.

"Wayne, you'll have to primer this whole car again if you want any kind of finish."

He nodded and crammed his hands in his back pockets. "Well, it's yet another part of my life that runs around half-done."

It was the first note of self-pity she had heard from him, and she still had enough beer in her to feel a rush of sentiment—she knew about things that felt half-finished. Sandy lived on forty acres, what was left of a larger tract that had been Coker land since after the War of 1812, when it was granted to a veteran in the clan. Her father left only a daughter, so one day the land might no longer be called Coker Farm. With her father gone, upkeep was hers alone, and what once seemed manageable now felt as immovable as a hillside.

Walking toward the barn, she was about to whistle for the horses, but in the pink of evening they were already loping up the pasture. In the twilight the barn and stables didn't look so run-down. The trailer and yard appeared tidy, with cannas sprouting in her flower beds and jonquils blooming. She had nothing to be ashamed of. Anyway, Wayne had no right to judge her, driving such a car and living in the ratty motor court on 71B where you could rent by the month at a rock-bottom rate. So many men working the road like Wayne lived four or five to a room in squalor, then raced home on weekends to what family they could keep. To her, it was an unimaginable way to live, though she saw them come and go, prosper sometimes, and most survived year after year.

At the stable, the bay, brown, and black heads of the three horses nodded, happily waiting. Aloof, there was Trick of Light. Even in the evening, you could see the musculature of her neck and the firm glow of her brown body, the magical, delicate bounce of her fetlocks, pastern, and heel. Each step was a dance. She by far outclassed her stablemates.

Wayne held out his hand to Trick, and without

hesitation she bumped it with her muzzle, then flopped her lips on his upturned fingers.

"You're a natural," Sandy said. Even after the walk she still felt beery and warm as if her head were stuffed with cotton and her heart suspended on a bounding thread.

"This is quite a horse," he said.

Sandy stepped to the opposite side of Trick's neck and caressed the animal's cheek. "She's no Ruffian, but if you follow the racing form, it's amazing to me how solid any issue of Phone Trick will run."

"Did she run?"

"Did she ever. She took a bad step one race, though, just after Daddy died."

"I'm sorry," Wayne said. She wasn't sure if he meant her father's death or the horse's injury. He patted the thoroughbred's shoulder and ran a hand down her barrel. "You going to breed her?"

"We'll see." She stuck her chin at the stables. "We got to make things comfortable in there to bed them down. There's a shovel by the door."

He took the broad-bladed shovel and was soon busy in the first stall. She began to rake down new hay, but found herself casting glances at him. He was diligent, pushing the wheelbarrow to each door, working rapidly without banging or loud scraping. It was clear to her he was no newcomer to a stable. It pleased her, too, that like her father and her people in the Arkansas Ozarks, this man from the upper Ozarks didn't press for sad details or drag out the condolences the way people in Hot Springs had when she had buried her father. When he passed her with the wheelbarrow, she fought the rush of familiarity that came over her. But soon he was beside her again.

"Have another pitch fork?"

She nodded at the rack at the back of the stable. They finished the last stall together, and he began to scoop feed into the pails as she led the animals in one by one.

When they finished, they stood watching the horses eat.

"You had horses in Missouri?"

"Mom and Dad did. Can't manage it now." He looked at her squarely.

She was sober now after the work, and just tired enough not to be eager to learn what he would want next, what he might angle for. And, since becoming a lead inspector, she never slept with a man on the job she was charged to monitor. Never.

"I want to thank you for a chance to see your farm."

She nodded.

He waited a moment. He would show right now, she thought, what kind of man he was and what he thought of her. Goliath, she thought, and remembered his swagger.

"Why don't you walk me to my car?"

Not what she expected but there was still time. At the car he lit a cigarette. She shook out a Marlboro, which he lit, and they both leaned against the Camaro's trunk and watched the comet for a while. She found herself looking at his lean face in the starlight. Wearing a ball cap all day did not mat his hair down quite as badly as it did other men's. He likely earned plenty and could keep a room separate from other workers. She imagined it was neat and spare and that he didn't go to sleep without a shower.

"Did you expect something different?" she asked.

He shook his head. "I didn't know." He looked at her, and to do this he was looking down. She was not often around men so tall. Her father had been a short, wire of a person just like Sandy. "But I really wanted to see. And not just a horse," he added.

"Right. You disappointed?"

"Not yet," he said. He pulled the cap from his back pocket and squared it on his head, shook his keys out of his front pocket.

"Well, thanks, though." She stopped, wanting to say more.

He nodded, then opened the car door and sat down in the Camaro and started the engine. It was loud and powerful. Quickly it smoothed out.

She stood with her arms crossed, but relented and gave him a slight wave. With a nod he pulled out, slowed at the cattle guard, then she shut the gate behind him.

Later that week, dusk nearing, Sandy drove the troubled frontage road to the Yarberry's and was surprised to see Wayne's green company pickup parked against the A-frame. That dog, she thought, honing in on a lonely wife whose husband won't be back till nine if he is back at all tonight. She swung the carryall around the cul-de-sac and backed it into a gravel access secluded by cedar brush and sassafras whips.

From her glove box she pulled out one of the new battery-operated hand levels with a 5X scope. Despite the crosshair, the hand level gave a clarified and enhanced picture of the yard and A-frame. A black metal rectangle that fit in her hand and weighed no more than an apple, the device was new enough to her that she still reveled in its magic. It seemed to draw together all the light in whatever quadrant was gazed on so that every movement and detail stood out in what was framed by the lens. It pained her, but only for a moment, to remember the one-night stand that had won her this instrument off a bridge inspector. The level was rightful treasure, proper tribute due the one who endured the vision of the bridge inspector's hairy bottom the next morning and his stupid guilt at not remembering a thing.

The lens revealed a Maurer backhoe parked for the night with its blade shoved in the dirt. From the look of things, some work on the new driveway had commenced. Wayne pulled a large blue cooler from the back of his truck and opened it on the ground for Mrs. Yarberry, who held her little daughter on her hip. Mother and daughter leaned to peer at the cooler's contents, which Sandy could not see. Wayne shut the cooler and carried it to the front porch with some struggle.

For a while Wayne stood with the mother and daughter, the adults talking and laughing a bit. From his gestures, Wayne seemed to be telling a fishing story. He was not standing too close, and as she watched through the scope, Sandy felt suspicion ebb into curiosity. Then the tyke wriggled in her mother's arms and reached out to Wayne. A life without a daddy much of the time would be a confusing hardship.

Wayne took the child up as if it were natural to him and began to motion at the backhoe and around the yard with his free hand as he bounced her. The little one, clearly delighted, buried her face in Wayne's hair.

When Wayne returned the child and climbed back in his truck, Sandy hesitated, then started the carryall and pulled it to the edge of the steep driveway. As Wayne topped the drive he stopped. His window was already down and he leaned out from it without wariness or guilt, his expression flat and his eyes showing the only hint he was surprised to see Sandy.

"I see you have a backhoe down there," Sandy said. "Is she satisfied?"

"Not yet, but she will be," he said, probably picking up on her double meaning.

"Oh?" Sandy asked. "That the plan? What was in the cooler?"

He sat back in the car seat, and in the shadow of the cab it was clear from his eyes he was giving Sandy a cold, second assessment. "Me and some of the boys caught a mess of fish the other night in that pond that we're going to drain by the quarry. They were too many."

Sandy raised her eyebrows. "She wants fish?"

Wayne's forehead creased and he leaned out of his window towards her. His voice dropped, and this made his words seem even more annoyed with her. "Did you not hear her say so when you had her going about her husband off working that tunnel and what she missed?" He watched her a bit as she tried to recall. "Maybe you ought to listen more and suspect less," he said. Then he put the truck in gear and eased past her and drove away.

Though the weather was chill, spring rains started, gray skies and mists that lasted the entire day. The cut became too slick and the earth too heavy and clasping by afternoon, and the crews traipsed off merrily to bars and trouble. Silt built up down in the box culverts, and the pits dug to hold it back from tributaries of White River filled, then overflowed. Landowners downstream began complaining. At the Maurer trailer, a bevy of green pickup trucks were parked outside. When Sandy eased her white carryall into the gravel lot, she fretted at her lack of enthusiasm for a confrontation. This usually was her favorite terrain: spying a problem on the job and getting the money-hungry contractor to hop on messes it was ignoring. She sat with the carryall running, windshield wipers yawping, and was bothered that she knew which of the hunter green Ford trucks was Wayne's by its scratches and the white plate on the back with its four black numbers, 6459.

She pulled open the trailer door and what had been laughter died down quickly. Unlike the state trailer, where under bright fluorescent lights survey crews gathered to eat and crew chiefs checked math in their surveyor's log books, Maurer kept its trailer as dark as a barroom, and yet spotless inside. There was something sinister about this. With such cleanliness and seeming efficiency on the surface, what was there to hide in here in the dark? All of Maurer's foremen waited—Wayne, the dirt foreman, the bridges foreman, box culverts, the machinist's foreman in his black, greasy hat with its long leather flap covering the back of his neck. And the lead foreman, Andy, an older man with navy tattoos, an ex-submariner Sandy had learned. From his damp, clay-streaked face

Wayne's eyes shone out like shards of gun metal.

"What do you need, Sandy?" he asked.

It threw her that it was Wayne asking, not the lead foreman, who had yet to speak a word to her in his two weeks on the job. The other foremen stood, arms crossed over their bellies and chests, as if Wayne were in charge.

"You got a problem," she said.

Silence from them. Someone's body odor stunk powerfully in the close, dark trailer. What was it with these Missourians? There was never any fun or banter when more than one of them faced her.

"The barrow pits at the exeunt to every box culvert on this job, they need cleaning. They've topped and are leaking silt into White River, and I got landowners bitching."

Still silence. On the floor, water dribbled, one of the foremen was so rain soaked.

"You surveyed them?" Wayne asked.

Finally some levity. "Have them cleaned out, Wayne."

He shook his head. "Survey them. Then I'll clean them out."

"What do you need them surveyed for? They're a standard pay item. They go so much a pit. Zip! You muck it out, and it's on next week's pay schedule."

In the dim light, she could see the tips of gray teeth, one foreman smiling. They were enjoying the spectacle of a small woman getting riled.

"That other bunch of monkeys. They sunk those pits. Did they keep up with them?"

She moved toward him and could feel the valence within the semicircle of men push against her. "I wouldn't recommend following their lead."

Wayne raised his chin and stroked under it, eyeing her. She could hear his thumb crackling against stubble under his neck. "And after they collapsed and left, what was it, a year and a half before the bid even let, and a winter at least before we come on the job?"

Her jaw was tightening and she was glad it was dark—maybe he couldn't read her expression.

She didn't understand where he was going with this.

"Wayne, it doesn't matter how many seasons this has been left undone," she said. "A pit can only get so full, and then the excess washes out. That's what's happening now. That's why I got folks downstream upset." She felt as if she were talking into a dry well, cold and stony on the way down and no echo coming back. There he stood in the semicircle of his men, his eyes like a mirage of water hoped for but not there.

"Survey them full," he said. "I'll muck them out. Then you survey them empty. I don't know the volume, and I want it on a spreadsheet. Anything we move, you measure."

After a moment the lead foreman pulled out a can of Copenhagen and snapped his thick fingers thrice against its metal lid. There seemed something final in that motion, like a gavel rapping.

Outside she gripped the cracked steering wheel of the carryall. She had just acquiesced to something that was going to cost AHTD man hours, something that would raise questions down the line from the Springdale office to Fort Smith, maybe all the way to Little Rock. She backed the carryall out slowly and quietly as if nothing in the world were the matter and she surely didn't want to stir something up, not Sandy.

The weather dried and turned hot and sunny, a harbinger of summer. Sandy met one of the department's survey crews on a pretty part of the cut that overlooked a slope of tall rye grass so vast you could see wind push down blades of browning rye in snakes of undulating shadow. The survey gunner bent to the theodolite with his AHTD ball cap backwards, a big dip of snuff muddling the numbers he read to the crew chief who recorded them in her orange survey booklet.

"Okay," the crew chief's voice rang down the slope to where two rodmen with levels were measuring the muck Maurer was to clear from the mouth of a box culvert. The rodmen wore rubber hip waders and sometimes sank thigh deep in red silt.

"I can't believe they want us to survey this," the crew chief said to Sandy. She shielded her eyes from the sun. "This is a nasty waste of time."

"Wayne won't crank an engine without some spreadsheet on it," Sandy said. She was focused on what looked like a scuffle in the middle of the cut where a ditch crew was supposed to be working. They were the real dregs on the job, a subcontractor from Springfield that Maurer had brought down.

"Wayne?" the crew chief asked. Like Sandy, the crew chief was a woman, and out here that was rare, other than flagmen and sign holders. They looked out for each other.

Sandy did not even realize she had used his first name. "Maurer's dirt foreman. A real pistol," she added, glad she was already too suntanned to show any blush.

"Maybe you finally met your match," the crew chief said with a sly look up from her numbers.

SANDY AND WAYNE

"Okay," she hollered to her rodmen.

"What the hell is going on down there?" Sandy asked, hoping the ditch crew might provide distraction from any more talk about Wayne.

The gunner shifted the theodolite, a sophisticated survey gun that could hone in on a shirt button half a mile away. He spit. "Damn. One fellow's holding another up by his feet and bouncing his head on the ground."

He backed away and motioned Sandy to the eyepiece. Framed in the scope, one of the tall, bearded rowdies from the ditch crew held another crew member, a smaller, older man, up by his boots and was shaking him while the others helped. The bearded fellow was the ditch foreman. The old man, the one being shaken, was a notorious drunkard.

"Come on people," said the crew chief. "It's a ditch crew. I don't care if they get paved over. My guys are down there drowning in slime."

Sandy turned away from the gun and gave the survey crew chief a stare.

A green Maurer truck boiled across the cut and stopped near the ditch crew. Wayne hopped out. The gunner was still watching the fracas. "Now we'll see some sand," he said.

Whatever Wayne said to the ditch crew, the tall ditch foreman lowered the old man to the ground. Then Wayne and the crew huddled around the old man.

"I don't think he's breathing," the gunner said. He spit. "Somehow I don't think that was a fight. No, that weren't any fight. He's real still, that old coot is."

The crew chief whacked his hind end hard with her orange book. "Quit that and shoot me some numbers. That's not any of our concern down there."

Back in his truck Wayne came racing up the slope to Sandy and the survey crew. He leaned out the window. "Any you all know CPR?" he hollered.

"Get on the radio," Sandy said to the survey crew chief. "Get an ambulance out here." She hurried to Wayne's truck, pushed aside blueprints, and climbed in.

"You know CPR, then?" Wayne asked as they slammed and bounced back down to the ditch crew.

She nodded. She knew it from required training, but had only performed it for real once on her father when she found him in the stable. Then it had been too late.

The ditch crew parted and Sandy kneeled. The old drunk lay on the ground, a gray-bearded man with greasy, gray and white hair. He wore a stained yellow shirt that said, *Surf's Up!* A logo of the pitcher-shaped Kool-Aid man rode a surfboard above the old worker's pot belly. His face, which seemed part Mexican to Sandy, was a dark purple, and a strand of green vomit hung from one corner of his blue, cracked lips.

She took a breath and cupped the back of the old man's hair where cold sweat wetted her fingers. Over her, Wayne's shadow blocked the sunlight, and she waved him to one side. The old man wasn't breathing. She tilted his head back and his mouth dropped open. Pushing two fingers inside, she felt around in the gooey airway. Then she looked over his white tongue to where his uvula was pasted drily against one of his tonsils. There was nothing blocking his airway.

She pinched his nose and was bending down to deliver her first puff when Wayne grabbed her shoulder.

"I got one of them things you put between his mouth and yours." When he saw the confusion on her face, he added, "To keep off the AIDS."

"I didn't learn with nothing like that," she said, almost angrily. What he said didn't make things any easier. "You know how to use one?"

Wayne shook his head. "They just give me the equipment. No training."

"You start training right now."

Wayne knelt down beside her. She bent over the old man and swallowed. Then she took a breath and gripped the old man's chin with one hand and kept his nose pinched with the other.

She popped her mouth over his, feeling the scale on his lips, the slime at their corners, his whiskers needling her face. It took intense concentration to create a seal between her small mouth and his large, flaccid, dry lips—she flexed facial muscles she never considered. Do this right or he dies, she thought in a loop to battle her revulsion at the act, this embrace, a hideous kiss. She puffed hard, breathed in through her nose, puffed twice more. The old man's mouth was a cesspool of stale booze and vomit.

Raising up, she wiped her mouth and fought back a gag. It was a relief to see Wayne down on his knees there watching her. "Spread your palm out like this. Now put your other hand on it." She grabbed Wayne's hands and positioned the heel of Wayne's palm on the old worker's breastbone. "Now mash hard, thirty times and count out loud."

He started.

"Hard, I said."

The ditch crew gathered close as if ready

to defend their crewmate. Sandy leaned over to Wayne and whispered. "I am not shitting you. You should feel his ribs break. Harder," she said. "And stop at thirty."

Three more puffs and once again she fought the gag, but did not wipe her mouth. When she had drawn her hand across her lips on the first round, the stink and taste of the old man's sweat made her struggle even more difficult.

Wayne hit thirty and she breathed into the old man again. When she drew back, the ground seemed to lift and spin beneath her knees. She found herself kneading Wayne's shirt. "That's good, Wayne. Good. Now, if he comes to, the first thing he'll likely do is throw up. So be ready to turn him with me fast."

On her next cycle, on her third puff, she felt a gurgle start deep in his throat and resistance blocking the breath she was forcing in him. She lurched back. "Help me, Wayne."

But he was already with her, lifting the old man to turn him away from Sandy and onto his side. The old worker gasped, and then retched, not violently, but with a miserable, slow steadiness born of exhaustion.

Sandy patted between the old man's shoulder blades while Wayne balanced him. Wayne was watching her, his eyes wide, his face slack.

"Just hold him like that," she said. "Hold him." She realized she was gripping Wayne's shoulder very tightly. She had no notion how long she had been doing so. She loosened her grip, but did not let go. The earth was still bucking under her.

When the old worker's eyes opened and he groaned, the ditch crew broke out in laughter and cheers, even some applause. Sandy should have felt relief, maybe satisfaction. She and Wayne had done it; they caught the old man in time.

The ditch foreman bent toward her. He was the one who had been shaking the old man upside down. "Lady, that was amazing. I mean, I tried. . . What's that poem? If the face is red, shake him on his head. Something like that?"

"Shut up," Sandy said. She stood up, her fists

clenched. "Shut up!"

"Jesus, what's with you, lady?" the ditch foreman asked.

Paramedics arrived and Wayne was explaining what Sandy and he had done.

"He's been drinking," the ditch foreman said to everybody gathered. "He's had nothing in his system but Ten High for five days straight."

One paramedic knelt down to the victim and sent the other to get an IV of B12.

"You were responsible for him," Sandy shouted at the ditch foreman. "He's an old man. Why'd you let him drink like that? Out in this sun!"

The foreman stood with his mouth open. "Lady, come on," he said.

"And you did exactly the wrong thing when he collapsed, didn't you?" She came at him. "You should have been taking care of him. What did they teach you up there?"

Wayne grabbed Sandy by the belt loops of her jeans just as she lunged at the ditch foreman, who was backpedaling. When one of the loops snapped, he gripped Sandy's waist with both hands just above her hips and held her fast, though she fought him in a rage.

"Get them medics his ID and radio 01 for his insurance," Wayne shouted at the ditch foreman. "And you get in this truck," he ordered Sandy, jerking her toward his vehicle.

He opened the door clumsily. When he forced her into the passenger's seat, he narrowly missed snagging her head on the doorframe. He opened the driver's side door and slammed it as he sat down. He started the truck and peeled down the cut for a great distance, then swerved to a stop. Dust rolled over the cab. The scene was behind them. The old man's fate was in the hands of the medics. Wayne shut off the engine.

"Now," he said, facing her. It was as if he knew.

She swung at him, struck his chest, waled at his arms. "Goddamn it, Wayne. Goddamn him. Goddamn it." She flailed away twice more until her swing lacked heart.

He caught both her wrists as her fists came

at him one last time. "Be still," he said firmly. "Be still, now. Settle it down."

When she began to sob, he wrapped his arms around her. Slowly he rocked her against him. His chest smelled of wet clay, his shirt of sweat and cigarettes.

"Be still," he said, holding her tight. "Be still, now. You did good. Real good, Sandy. You saved him. Be still."

In Maurer's trailer there were accident reports to fill out, his for the company and workman's comp, hers for the AHTD. The old worker's collapse happened late in the day. The jobsite wound down without her and Wayne. Her reports were more involved than his, and she was shaking. While she worked, Wayne sat stiffly in an old swivel chair watching the western sky. Though his blue eyes were wide open, he seemed meditative, and when the light shifted she saw runnels of muscle working along his jawline. What a shock this had been to both of them, and then she had gone and lost it in his truck. When the ditch foreman pulled up to the trailer, Wayne went outside and dealt with him. Through the thin metal walls of the trailer she could hear that the ditch foreman wanted to make some kind of big apology to her. Wayne sent him away.

"Thank you," Sandy said when he sat back down.

Wayne nodded. He knew when to be silent, and had been for some time now. He rose and began faxing the papers he had filled out, probably to Maurer headquarters in Sedalia. Suddenly that place no longer seemed so far away to her.

"Will this be a big headache for you?" she asked.

He shook his head. "He's stabilized at Washington Regional. He's with a subcontractor anyway. So it's their deal."

"They'll fire him, won't they? And he'll get stuck with a great big medical bill."

He shrugged. "I wish he was with Maurer. Old Man Maurer would take care of him, I'm sure. May have never let him get this bad. We watch that. But he's not ours."

She folded up her papers, then looked around in a daze until she realized her satchel was in her carryall still parked above the box culvert.

He handed her an envelope for her paperwork. "That's just it, Wayne. He don't belong to anybody. That asshole of a foreman should have been looking out for him." She pulled off her AHTD ball cap, so dusty, its navy blue seemed purple-red. She crumpled it on the countertop. "He's old, Wayne. They knew he was drinking too much."

"They got a job to do," Wayne said, squinting at her. "Tiny company like that doesn't come with a human resource manual." He watched her awhile. "You been at this long enough to know."

"I don't know, Wayne," she said. "Maybe I haven't been at this long enough." Never had she admitted anything like this to a contractor, but somehow with him after this just now, all the posturing seemed a waste. She scraped her ball cap along the countertop then clutched the hat in her lap.

"What you did, that was something else," he said. "We're lucky to have you here."

She let out a long breath and, agitated, looked around again. He tapped out a cigarette and handed it to her, then lit it.

"He's stable? He's okay?" she asked. Even the menthol wasn't so bad.

"He had a B12 seizure."

"Like a vitamin deficiency?"

Wayne shrugged. "I broke some of his ribs, like you said. But he's in better hands now than with that crew, don't you imagine?"

She gave a snort of laughter in which there wasn't any amusement. "Were you really worried about AIDS?"

He shook his head.

"You reckon I should worry?"

He pondered a bit. "That poor old man hasn't been interested in being intimate with anything outside a whiskey bottle in a long, long time."

"No family?"

"Listen, you need to quit thinking about this."

He gathered his hat and keys. "I know a bar in West Fork way off the job. I'd like you to let me take you for a drink. Then maybe we can see your horses."

When he neared her, she reached out and grabbed his hand, squeezed it for a moment. "Thank you for getting me out of that with the ditch foreman. And twice."

He smiled. "You were right pissed off earlier. Daddy used to send us out of the barn when we got that way."

The bar was the sort of dark dive only contractors could discover—a long, sheet metal countertop trimmed in scarred white oak, behind which there were three beer taps, all American. Near these waited a jar of hard-boiled eggs, pickled, glowing, and so still they seemed suspended in gelatin. Next to this sat another jar full of indecent sausages floating in a red emulsion. By the label these promised to be fiery hot. Not to lose pace with changing times, the poster behind the bar featured a blazing Latina passionately holding out a bottle of Budweiser. Something in Spanish was written in the sweat condensed across her dark thighs. Sandy looked around for Mexican poultry workers. But tonight it was only locals, folks from other hills far away from the Cokers, folks she didn't know. They took two bottles of beer to a table in the back and in silence watched others play shuffleboard and pool. Wayne bought her a pack of Marlboro Reds from a shambling cigarette girl wearing a grungy neck brace.

"What was your daddy like?" Sandy asked him.

In the dim light, Wayne's eyes seemed to focus on some distant point. "His people were Scots-Irish and part Osage." He sipped his beer. "Never laid a hand on us boys. Like I said, if one of us got fractious, he'd just look up and ask if we needed to leave the barn. We knew the answer."

"You turned out all right."

"I about didn't. I remember one night he caught me coming home in the dawn just when the birds start singing. All he said was, 'Wayne, I got to live in this town after you've done your damage and you're gone.' Once I knew I was letting him down, there was no more of that. I met with Old Man Maurer and been a wage earner ever since." He turned to her. "I bet your dad was proud of you."

"Astonished," she said. "I don't think he ever knew what to do with a daughter. Mom died, see. I was real young. By God, he let me make whatever I wanted of myself."

He carefully stripped the label off his wet bottle. "Then it wasn't him you were fighting back there? In the truck?"

She took out a cigarette but was rolling it between her fingers, staring at it. This was getting a little closer to the quick than she anticipated. "I didn't get to him in time, Wayne. Had a heart attack. Maybe I could have saved him I'm thinking now, like we did that old man." She put the cigarette to her lips, and he was right there with the lighter. Leaning back, she drew on the cigarette and felt tired, but sharpened with the nicotine in her. "Everybody ought to have somebody to help them. I was his help. And Daddy was mine. I didn't get there. I was working. And now. . . now I know what I could have done."

After a moment, Wayne nodded. They sat watching the barflies. She felt quite comfortable with him, and now they shared something frightening, something that could have meant death had they failed. But they hadn't failed. They had saved that old man for what good it did anybody. She worried and wondered at the ease she felt sitting with Wayne here sharing the end of such a wild day.

He set his bottle aside and pulled his ball cap off the table. "Let's go help those horses."

When they had the horses back in the stable and bedded down, she said, "Wayne, stay. Stay with me tonight."

After he showered, he came to bed. There was no asking, no bashful silliness. His body was as long and lean and hard as she imagined. They kissed and she tasted mouthwash. She was impressed that he had found it in the mess under the bathroom sink and was thoughtful enough to use it. How good it felt to be held, to have her face touched rather than being the one grabbing hair, positioning head and neck and chin to open a filthy airway. How cleansing to be kissed instead of being the one desperate to force a seal on crusted lips, around eroded and bleeding gums.

She pressed Wayne's shoulders down against the bedspread and eased on top of him. On his chest some of the hairs were gray. When she braced her palms against his pectorals, she thought of the old man, thought of what she had taught Wayne to do. Along the center of his chest, she traced the hardness of his breastbone, lingered on the spot where a palm would fit to start compressions. Instead of frailty there, she found firmness, like the transfer case to some powerful, invaluable machine. She did not want to think of him as wonderfully made, but there he was at her fingertips, and she was giving in.

He pushed her hair back and touched her cheek. His eyes were lovely looking at her, so light blue they seemed to have no depth, only a surface shine, like a gas burner's pure flame.

"What are you thinking?" she asked.

"Nothing, Sandy. Nothing. I'm just amazed. Just really amazed."

The next morning she reported to the Springdale AHTD headquarters to file her paperwork and waited in the conference room with four other lead inspectors, all men.

The survey crew chief who had witnessed the old man's collapse passed through the conference room. She cast Sandy a strange look that set Sandy's teeth on edge. She thought of Wayne's jawline in the evening sun, how it knotted with tension. One of the other lead inspectors spat a tawny strand of snuff into a Gatorade bottle brown with his chew, watching Sandy as he did. She crossed her legs and worked the hasps on her satchel.

When the chief engineer hollered a last name

that was not hers, she still did not relax. If it were known, what she had done last night with Wayne would mean her removal from AR 4005 and a suspension. It would be a long time, if ever, before she got a nod to be a lead inspector again.

There was a voice out in the lobby, one she didn't recognize. A Mr. Maurer was announced to the chief engineer and the door to the chief's office shut for many minutes.

"That one's yours, ain't it?" asked the tobacco chewer.

Before she could nod, the chief engineer's door opened. He asked for her softly, by her first name rather than her last.

She stepped inside the chief's office, her satchel bumping her knees awkwardly till she shouldered it.

The chief introduced Mr. Maurer, who was indeed old, tall, and thin. He stood to shake her hand, holding a straw cowboy hat against his slacks. He wore a short-sleeve, green golf shirt with the Maurer logo on the breast. His face was drawn and serious. The chief asked her to sit. When she did not spy her paperwork on the chief's desk, she felt suddenly as if she were a cub surveyor again holding the rod level while a semi bore down on her.

"Ms. Coker," Maurer began, "I want to thank you for what you did yesterday on our Greenland job."

She was still apprehensive, but she managed to say, "You're welcome, sir."

The chief engineer regarded her coolly. "Mr. Maurer drove from Sedalia, Sandy."

"I appreciate your coming. I know you're busy," Sandy said. Though it was cool and foggy outside the windows, the room closed warmly in on her.

"I understand you had the patience to teach Wayne Sheridan some CPR as well," Maurer said with a friendly smile. He had a tan, sun-wrinkled face, and his short, silver hair looked as if he had just come from the barber.

The clock ticked at the top of 7 a.m. "I

couldn't have done it on my own," she said, too timidly. She desperately wanted to rally herself, but cold sweat crawled down her ribcage.

"That Wayne is like a son to me, Ms. Coker." Maurer turned to the chief engineer as if for confirmation of something. "My two boys are of no account. But I raised Wayne in this business, in their stead, from before he left high school."

Sandy felt suddenly low and tawdry, as if she were faced with Wayne's father here and she had led the boy astray. Foolish to think this—what had happened was just two adults leaning on each other. But it did put her and Wayne in jeopardy with both of these men.

Into an awkward pause, the chief engineer said, "Good help is golden." He seemed to make a point not to look at Sandy.

"Help doesn't come close to the word for Wayne Sheridan," Maurer said, his voice rough with real emotion, as if it were a point of honor he acknowledged.

When the chief engineer nodded, everything

seemed settled, and Sandy was embarrassed to hear her breath exhale.

Mr. Maurer squinted at her. "Everything okay?"

She swallowed and sought frantically to talk about anyone other than herself, but her thoughts rushed like crows over rye, gabbling, never settling. "What will happen to that old man, the fellow who had the seizure?" Not where she intended to go, but it would suffice.

Mr. Maurer leaned back in his chair and crossed his arms over his chest. His forearms were dark and creased, like two banks of a dry river bed. "You're good help, Ms. Coker. What would you do about that?"

"He's old. He's going to be out of work. And that medical bill, with an ambulance ride, it'll be a whopper."

The chief engineer's frown was as fearsome as if he'd been forced to gulp a shot glass of red ink.

Mr. Maurer looked her up and down, then held her eyes for a minute. "Chief, you got good people here. Tell you what I'll do. I'll make sure that subcontractor does right. And if they don't, I'll sign him on with us, and we'll get it taken care of. That sound okay?"

Sandy nodded.

They rose and shook hands.

After Maurer left, the chief engineer shut the door, watched her for a bit. "Don't let that charity fool you. He's down here to make money, and so is this Wayne fellow."

She nodded.

"Do you need a day off?" he asked. "You look bad."

She shook her head.

When he showed her out, he hollered the last name of the next lead inspector on his shit list.

She had the fencing lady to check on, and a property owner on a tear about the renewed blasting, two survey books kicked back by Little Rock. So much else to do, anything between her and Wayne had to end, but she found herself bouncing the carryall down the cut to where he stood.

When she stopped the car, she looked for anything in the front seat she could carry to him, the specs, some blueprint to complain about. Maybe there was no sense shamming? "Damn," she whispered, and made a fist and pounded it against her thigh a couple times.

She closed the door and went to him empty handed. He smiled at her for an instant, but then his attention was back on the rovings of the scrapers and the crane and dump trucks. Down in the cut, a regular army of yellow, heavy machinery roared and grunted. They were his to command.

"What are you thinking when you look out on that mess?" Sandy asked. She wanted him to say something raunchy, something disappointing, something low and predictable. God, keep me away from this, she thought, her hand still in a fist. After this morning's encounter, surely that was enough to scare her. Yet here she was tripping after him like a schoolgirl.

"I used to think about cubic yards per hour versus the cost of fuel and labor." He wrinkled his nose, but kept his eyes on a front-end loader that had joined the machinery below. "Now spreadsheets track that for you."

"I didn't ask what you used to think."

He laughed and looked at her. "Well, I was just now thinking about this one part in the Bible where Isaiah says, 'Make straight in the desert a highway for our God.' How even way back then there was a Sandy and a Wayne and all these fools as well, raising highways, leveling hills, making straight the path for kings to ride on in chariots. Don't you reckon?"

She looked at him a long time and very much wanted to touch him, but that would bring this whole end of the jobsite to a halt.

"You read the Bible a lot?"

He watched a scraper make an awkward turn and lose traction, throwing clods from its massive tires high in the air. "Not anything but the Gideon and take-out menus to read in the hotel rooms."

She knew that to be true, but then why read anything after a day of this?

"They don't name them people who built highways in the Bible, do they?"

Wayne shook his head. "Lot of kings, though. Kings and queens and naughty switcheroos and lusty stuff, children in disguise, brothers thrown down holes. They had a ball back then before Jesus come along and got everybody straightened out."

When she didn't leave, his smile faded. Finally he turned to her with a sad look on his face, the first time she had ever seen him look sad. "I would like you to meet me at the Sam Hill Inn on 59. Tonight. If you want to."

They lay in bed at the Sam Hill Inn on the route to Sallisaw. It was growing dark, but she had no worries. She had fed and watered the horses on the way out of town, and a neighbor boy was coming to stable them. Though warmer weather made them indolent, the boy could handle them while she went to the races, or so she told his mother when she paid her.

"This could get bad, Sandy, me and you," Wayne said, stroking her hair. "This isn't what the dirt foreman and the lead inspector are supposed to be doing."

She told him about meeting Mr. Maurer and what was said.

He looked up at the ceiling and put both hands behind his head. He was a pleasant lover. Tender, slow, kind. She admired the muscles in his arms that buckled as he rested.

"I really don't want to let that man down, Sandy."

She sat up slowly, the cheap bed creaking. "I got people I don't want to let down either, Wayne. There's not a lot of women lead inspectors in the Arkansas Highway Department. You think how this might fall out."

He watched her as she talked, and though she still found his eyes a barrier, it pleased her how he listened or at least seemed to listen. Even pretending to pay attention would make him better than most of the men she had been with.

"What do you want to do?" he asked.

She clutched a pillow to her chest and looked straight ahead. The room seemed darker, and through the thin hotel walls came the whispers and howls of the highway at night. "Just exactly what we're doing," she said.

Spring was nearly over and there were no takers for partnering with her for a foal out of Trick of Light. Greedy owners with studs standing wanted fees and not partnerships. Wayne encouraged her to hold out for next season. She was tempted to see if one of her father's old trainers might take Trick on and win a few, but by the time they could have her in shape, Trick would have to ship so far away—Fairmount Park, Louisiana Downs, or tattered Evangeline Downs—worlds away from Hot Springs.

On the job she and Wayne were careful and rarely if ever alone. When they gathered with others on the Maurer crew, she hoped no one noticed how the two of them never addressed one another, never met one another's eyes. With the bridge foreman, the drainage crews, the seed man, and the fencing lady, Sandy battled stupidity, greed, waste, and negligence. But of the earthwork she had no complaints. This she found troubling. Yet Wayne's work moved more steadily and cohesively than dirt work on any other jobsite she had inspected. Was she being lax on the fill as the dirt approached grade? Was she turning a blind eye to what Wayne did with topsoil or drainage? Questions, doubts dogged her. Still, as she recorded the progression—460 + 00 to 1050 + 00, lanes raised, fine grading commenced—she could see it would soon end. The numbers and days would meet in the diary at the end of the job and there would be no more need for a dirt foreman.

On more and more weekends he did not drive back to Sedalia. He left the Camaro parked at the motor court and sometimes rented a car, or walked to The Limelight Lounge or to the back of a nearby IGA store where she picked him up.

SANDY AND WAYNE

They rode horses all weekend until he knew her acreage well. They fished in White River and made a home of the trailer. Trick of Light grew restive on weekends when he was away. It was too homey and at the same time too precarious.

He was never demanding, knew when she was too tired, could read what she wanted as well as he could the horses—Old Dan, the large gelding he rode, and Little Anne, her favorite for long rides. What they had together, Sandy and Wayne didn't acknowledge with *I love you* or long embraces and passionate kisses. It was as if the twin pressures of AR4005 ending, or the two of them being caught and a scandal erupting, kept them from discussing any future. Even when they were riding on her land, or shooting in some dark pool hall away from Greenland, or holding each other at the Sam Hill Inn, they had only so long together and couldn't bear to clutter precious time with reality, with the inevitable. And time was flying. Summer came, and she watched Maurer's progress with foreboding and hated marking its achievements on the wall chart tracking each job in the Springdale office.

When her mobile phone rang from an unknown caller ID, she usually didn't pick up. The emergency phone was state property and not publicly listed. But on an August morning she pulled it from its black case and answered, "Coker, AR 4005."

"Is this that lady with the Highway Department?"

"Mrs. Yarberry?"

"I need you to be here right now." Shrill the voice.

She raced along the freshly striped frontage road and easily found the new driveway down to the A-frame. She forced herself to slow and pull up to the house cautiously in case the toddler or the dog might be running about. The driveway was smooth and long, easy to navigate, and Sandy calmed herself by thinking that Wayne and Maurer had done right by this woman.

Mrs. Yarberry was in the yard standing stiffly. Blood was dripping down her arms. Otherwise her face and skin were sheet white. Sandy opened the carryall door very slowly.

"Is your husband home?"

Mrs. Yarberry stared at her, and Sandy could hear that the young mother was making a noise like a steam valve losing pressure, a high, insistent whine. Her teeth were clenched. Both of her forearms were mauled and bleeding. On her face were wounds that looked like a range of purple mountains in some awful, oriental-style drawing.

When Sandy drew closer, she saw the toddler on the ground just behind the mother, face down, in a pink sundress. Her plump hands were balled into fists. If she weren't so still, Sandy would have thought she was throwing a tantrum.

Sandy swallowed and realized how humid it was down in the valley here by the house with that preposterous frontage road blocking any breeze. The baby wasn't moving.

Trying to keep control, she looked to the clothesline where the animal had been, the wolf. It wasn't there, but then she saw a furry, gray heap lying in a clearing some ways off. An axe handle stuck up from its abdomen.

Sandy jolted. The young mother was right next to her. Mrs. Yarberry had snuck up on her, and was standing there with her teeth grinding.

"My arms are broken. I can't pick her up," she said. Her voice sounded as if she were trapped on a frozen lake and shaking with cold.

Sandy took a deep breath and knelt down by the child. On her knees, through her jeans, she could feel that the earth beneath the child was boggy and warm. The child would bleed out by the time an ambulance arrived.

"I killed that thing but it broke my arms," Mrs. Yarberry said in monotone.

"Lady," Sandy said, "I want you to get in the carryall if you can. Will you do that, please?" Sandy had her eyes closed tight. The air was as still and hot as the outside of a blast furnace. Up in the leaves a bush katydid sizzled.

Sandy heard the woman's feet shuffle away, then heard her cry out and curse. The car door slammed. Biting her lip, Sandy opened her eyes to take one long look at the baby and get her bearings. The baby wasn't moving. Red curls matted. Such a tiny neck.

Sandy squeezed her car keys twice in her hand. Then she scooped the child up and clutched the babe to her chest and ran for the carryall.

When she sat in the driver's seat, she felt the world lurch back and forth a few times. Her arms were slick and red and her shirt was dripping and pressed tight against her bra and stomach. It took everything she could muster to look only at the ignition, and then only at the dusty black slot where the key belonged, and fit it in and turn it. Her fingers slipped.

They flew down the drive, out the frontage road, to the interstate, off the exit ramp, and then into Fayetteville traffic. It was the lunch rush on Highway 71B. She drove aggressively, flicked on her hazard lights. Why was it still so hot? This baby wasn't moving.

"I'm going to Washington County Regional," Sandy heard herself saying.

Someone blared a horn at her.

The mother said nothing, but sat with her eyes shut tight and her arms stiff beside her, her stained palms flopped open on the seat.

Sandy wanted to use the horn, to mash it again and again and get these clods out of her way. But the child weighed on her. With her hands slick on the wheel, every perilous move, every advance or downshift of the gears on the column required an extra notch of concentration. "Lady, don't you want to hold your baby?" Sandy asked.

The mother arched her back but kept her arms still and her eyes closed, and Sandy thought she might be having a seizure.

"Lady?" Sandy couldn't believe it, but she felt her lips curling up in a smile and the more she fought it, the harder her lips bowed. Why try to be sweet to this poor woman? The woman had turned off the air conditioner; that's why it was so hot. Mrs. Yarberry had managed to get the passenger door open, buckle herself in, and then for some crazy reason she had switched off the air conditioner. And she had said her arms were broken. A warm soup glued Sandy's thighs to the seat. "Please, lady, won't you hold your baby?"

Traffic grew chaotic, and in the hot carryall the smell of blood became so strong it left a taste like salt and exploded gunpowder on every breath she took. A pickup cut her off; then from the emergency turn lane a luxury car swung up beside her. The driver flipped her the bird and was shouting. When she pulled the wheel, her elbows pinched the baby, which was as still and heavy as a sack of concrete.

When the blood soaked through her jeans and pressed Sandy's underwear against her skin, she jerked the carryall onto the shoulder and slammed it to a stop.

"I can't drive like this." She ground the gears into reverse, and last into park. Then she turned to the mother who had both eyes open and was staring out over the hood of the carryall with a look like she was about to leap through the windshield. Everything was stopped. They were at a stop, Sandy said to herself, but thought maybe she said it aloud as well. She glanced down.

Blood wasn't moving. No bubbles, no trying to get air. There was nothing left at the throat to breathe with. The baby was face up in her lap, blue eyes wide open in terror. Sandy could see knots of the baby's spine and maybe a remnant of the voice box and larynx down in where the skin ought to have covered.

Something was banging in the car. It took Sandy a long time to recognize it was her own left hand clawing at the crank to the window.

When she managed to get the window down, she took a deep breath and held it a while. "It won't do any good in the world for us to drive this baby to Washington Regional," she said. She closed her eyes, but the redness of the summer sun spread the image of the baby right back there. She glanced at the mother.

When Mrs. Yarberry caught Sandy's eyes, the mother began to thrash with all her might against the seat belt and door, the dashboard, the passenger's side window, which she cracked and spider webbed, her arms flailing, her breathing like an animal's on the run, teeth set on edge, flopping and thrashing until with a lunge she slammed her head against the hard steel loop that held the shoulder belt up. She slumped and settled, eyes closed, body pressed into the corner against the passenger's door as if a cyclone pushed her there.

A state trooper's cruiser, blue lights whirling, pulled onto the shoulder behind them. Relieved, Sandy felt adrenaline draining from her so rapidly, it was as if she sat in an ice cold downpour.

"We've had our fit now," Sandy said, her voice dry. She badly wanted a cigarette.

The mother nodded, her pitiful face mashed against the seat back. She was just beginning to cry. The state trooper rose very slowly from his cruiser.

When Sandy's lips parted, they made a sound like paper tearing, she was so parched. "Lady, I want you to reach over to me and take your little baby and hold her now, because here in a minute you aren't ever going to get to hold her again."

As if awakened from foolishness with a good slap, the mother opened her eyes and unbuckled her seat belt. With palsied hands, she reached into Sandy's lap.

It was then that Sandy closed her eyes and bit her lip, for the child did not come loose easily. It stuck to Sandy's legs and stomach until the whimpering young mother pulled hard and freed the corpse.

The officer stood at the open window with his jaw dropped, his sunglasses in his fist. Along his neck and cheeks there crept a hint of green.

"My name is Sandy Coker," Sandy heard

herself saying, "and I am the lead inspector for the Arkansas Highway and Transportation Department on Job AR4005. Greenland to West Fork."

She was standing on the ridge with her face buried in Trick's neck when she heard Wayne's Camaro rumble up, rattle at the cattle guard, then come on quickly. Along the western sky an orange and peach swath was mingling with crimson and then the navy blue heat of first night. The gloaming, her father used to call it. And there at the peak of the sky's roundest part, the strange comet hung like a chalk line snapped too hard, an amateur's first try at true and level. Trick of Light seemed to watch the comet as well. Sandy could hardly reckon how long they had stood out here, how long since she had saddled Trick. She recalled a clock face in the trailer reading 5:01 p.m., but what came after that? When had she dismounted? Where had they been riding? Such a patient filly, it made her wonder how diluted the Phone Trick was in her bloodline. Maybe too weak to foal any winners.

Wayne moved behind Sandy, hesitated, then wrapped his long arms around her waist. Though this was exactly what she had wanted him to do, in his arms she felt suddenly thin, like a filament in a bulb, ready to snap and flare to nothing the instant the switch was thrown.

"AHTD sent that boy, Allan, the redhead from Altus who sunburns so bad," Wayne said. "He did just fine filling in for you."

The whiskers on his chin scraped the top of her scalp—he was watching the comet. "You two look real peaceful up here."

She ran a hand down the tendons of his arm and saw a flash of the baby's spine again. "Wayne, I don't want you to say anything more. Nothing more tonight." Then she held tight to his arms to show him what she meant, what she needed.

In silence they walked Trick of Light to the barn, fed, and watered her. Without a word, without showers, without a drink, they climbed into bed, and she rode him in slow, deep circles, digging her nails into his chest as if she meant to crack him open and plant something there for all time.

That next morning they began a talk she had been dreading. It was so early that the light outside was the reverse of when it had left them, rising in the east now, the same color bands flipped to a different horizon. Mocking birds scolded a prowling barn cat.

"So when AR4005 ends, what'll you do, Wayne?"

He paused, about to take a drink of his coffee. Early in the mornings, his eyes darkened to the teal that comes at the bottoms of very deep springs. He was wearing a yellow shirt from Missouri, one of its colleges, with a cartoon bear swimming on it.

"I'm hoping Maurer will get that job south of the tunnel to build from Altus to Alma." He took a sip and his eyes seemed to focus and grow light like crystal hardening in a cave. "We can do it, too, Sandy. You watch. When I get that equipment marshaled, there'll be no outbidding us."

"You seem mighty sure."

He smiled.

"I'd like you to be really sure, Wayne." She said this with more neediness than she had intended, more than she had wanted to show.

No longer smiling, he sat down at the oak table with her. "You ever worry we'll get found out?"

"If we do, I'll just get a reprimand and get assigned on some other job, but we'll both be around here." It gave her pause to realize this affair, that Wayne meant enough to her that she could shrug off never being a lead inspector again. But there she had just done it.

He pushed his mug forward. "Listen. It

wouldn't be so easy on my end. Andy and Old Man Maurer.... Well, it's this way. If I were some no account on a ditch crew, well fine. But I'm not. Andy would see this as putting the whole operation in jeopardy. So would Old Man Maurer." He drew the mug back to him. "I can just hear what he would say, how it's not what did happen, but what people might think could happen. I mean, you sign off on every pay item on that job. Lead inspector." With a finger he made a swirling signature in the air. He paused a moment, and it was clear from his struggle and energy that he had been thinking about all this a very long time.

"We've never been blackballed anywhere," he went on. "And even if not that, there's no money in working a job when a Highway Department gets all up in your business and suspicious of something like ... well, like us. Like they might think we are."

He was thoughtful at least and talking sense, though she was pained hearing it.

"If you all get the job after the tunnel I might

very well not be the lead inspector there," Sandy offered. "That's the Alma office. It's their district." She feared every word she brought out, afraid the talk might slip quickly into anger, hurt, and confusion. But Wayne seemed steady enough to study where they were and what she was saying.

"I'm not sure it changes things entirely. But, yeah, you wouldn't be mixed up in the money and the inspecting."

She avoided looking at him and focused instead on the small, tin salt and pepper shakers her dad had been so fond of and the yellowed doily her mother had crocheted. She could feel Wayne watching her. "What if you don't get the bid?"

"Mr. Maurer takes his forces back up toward Rolla. There's a lot of work going on in Missouri that we have under contract, and more to bid on, too."

"You could work for a company down here, Wayne. Any Arkansas outfit would have you."

He shook his head. "Arkansas is a right-to-work state. They couldn't touch what I'm making."

He looked so intently at her she felt Arkansas's meanness was entirely her fault. "I'm not bragging. It's just facts."

She nodded and they were still for a long time. In a way this was more difficult than any discussion she recalled with any former lover, in that Wayne was not a liar and a tramp out to use her. So many of the men she had been with were of no account. Now him. He was golden, and it could slip away.

"I got years with the company, Sandy. Straight out of high school. Mr. Maurer himself taught me everything."

She raised her palm from the tabletop, and he went silent. She did not care for where this was going, but logic, which is no solace, predicted every turn of it. They were no longer looking at one another as they spoke. Both kept their eyes on the tabletop, and if they looked up it was only for a pained instant.

"Come on up there with me," he said. "I'll show you around. You'll like Sedalia."

She shook her head. "I'm here, Wayne. I got a retirement coming in just ten more years. And I got this land, and Trick of Light, and maybe foals next season. We aren't kids."

She caught his eyes and they were as clear as they became on the job when earth was moving and scrapers and dozers, dump trucks, and cranes shuttled all at once.

She almost whispered, afraid that saying it would shatter everything and he would leave right then and there. Lesser men would have left, and she was not yet entirely sure of him. "I'm looking for something here. Something that says I'm going to last. I need me someone I can count on."

After a while he firmed up his jaw. "Can we say we aren't going to solve this now?"

Way off on the highway, a big rig closed its jake brake and growled coming down one of the inclines. "This may not work out like we want," she said.

From the tabletop, he raised his hand and

showed her the lime-hardened white crust along his palm.

In the next few weeks, he asked her only once about the Yarberry baby. They were on the horses waiting for some ATVs to clear out of the valley so they could cross White River in peace. On the ATVs were children, far too young to be unsupervised on vehicles so prone to flip, so fast and dangerous.

"After what you seen," Wayne began, "with that poor baby, do you want one of your own, Sandy?"

The question was so big, it just hung there.

"You did say you wanted something lasting with you here," he added.

One of the children wound the throttle madly, and Little Anne pranced in agitation until Sandy settled her. "Part of me wants to. Just to have something that lasts."

She paused and could not help but think of

the agony a mother would endure watching her boy careening along, barely clinging to that horrible ATV. On Old Dan, Wayne tensed in the saddle, straightening his long legs in the stirrups, his eyes riveted on the boys, as if he, too, had seen enough damage this year to worry.

"But after what happened, Wayne, I swear, another part of me couldn't stand the pain of even one-tenth of what I saw if she had been my baby." The ATVs crossed White River without mishap, leaving the water tan with silt. Wayne stuck his chin at the trail. Now that the boys were safe and gone, he seemed relaxed on Old Dan. With the row of oaks along the ridge behind him, and the dappled light of early afternoon so yellow on his chest and arms, it seemed he belonged there on that old horse, in her country.

One weekend morning in late summer, she was scraping a pan sullied from some ill-advised, late-night snack Wayne had cooked them. Friday night they had too many beers in a Goshen bar with a wonderful juke box that played Hank Sr., and Patsy, and Johnny, and Willy, and even three old chestnuts from Tom T. Hall. For the first time, just before last call, she and Wayne danced, and it was to one of the Old Storyteller's slowest numbers.

Her hands, thin, tiny, and sun creased, shocked her emerging from the sudsy water. Brown, knotted, they were like the gnarly roots of the dwarf fruit trees her dad had been so enthused about near the end of his life.

Holding them out of the water, the faucet still gushing, she had a flash of herself on top of Wayne in the wee hours. But rather than a glimpse of ecstasy and delight, she saw a thin woman, neck and arms ravaged by the sun. She saw herself dry and wiry, wringing everything she could out of the man beneath her.

She slammed the faucet off so forcefully, the trailer shuddered.

Out the kitchen window, up on a hill, she saw Wayne standing in the morning sun. Very still, and her heart caught with worry that something was wrong.

Trick of Light loped up the hill to him, but he didn't acknowledge her, just stood with his head down. Though Sandy could not see for sure, she thought Wayne's eyes were shut. All of Trick's body language slowed in tempo, heightened in ceremony, as if she were a Lipizzaner or one of those creepy counting horses at the state fair about to perform. Whatever was going to happen, Sandy knew it was something Wayne and Trick had done before, something the horse enjoyed.

Wayne clasped his hands in front of him about belt high and looked like a Baptist praying in church. With one last high step, Trick bumped Wayne's ear with her muzzle. Next, she dropped her head over his shoulder and inched forward until her throat latch rested on his collarbone. Then—and this Sandy could clearly see—Trick of Light closed her eyes and the two stood there in the sunlight like mournful statues.

After a minute or two the scene was too much for her. When had he had time to teach the filly to do that? Or damn it, had it just happened naturally, when Trick saw Wayne was the right height and so she plunked her head there one night and found it soothing and knew she could come back to him and do the same again? Such an intense communion, like one of those silly, velvet paintings that are peddled on horse-struck girls, but there it was happening on her hillside. Wayne hadn't said a word that Trick would do this. Sandy knew she and Wayne, horse people, attached great significance to these quirks. Horses, though, just knew pleasure and sought it out, like they sought water or sunlight.

Attraction was so treacherous. Down in the sink, her fingers puckered, the skin going dead white and slightly blue. All at the same time, she wanted to march up that hill and tell Wayne to gather his shit and get on back where he belonged. And just as much she wanted to call him to her. She wanted to unlatch the window in front of her and raise it, and holler out, "Wayne. Come in here. I need you." And then she wanted to see him turn away from every distraction. She wanted to see him come striding for her.

One morning in the fall, recording progress on the wall chart, she heard her last name hollered from the chief's office.

She sat down. He shut the door.

"I had a real funny conversation with one of your old enemies," the chief said.

"Oh?"

"You remember Maxwell, that lead foreman at Rust who bragged so much about being a Notre Dame graduate?"

The chief smiled and busied himself with a stack of asphalt tickets. "Well, APAC Arkansas has hired him. He was real burnt up to hear how well Maurer is making out on his old jobsite."

"I reckon he would be." She fought down any urge to brag on Maurer.

"He was crass enough to suggest that after you'd been such an icy bitch to Rust you were now in bed with Maurer." The chief paused, and Sandy felt her forehead itch and burn. "His words, not mine. Can you believe the gall?"

"Leon, they were terrible people, and Max was the worst. I got the paperwork to back up every decision, every damn thing that happened."

"I know," he said, watching her, the pink tickets drooping in his hands. "I've been through every jot of that diary, then and now."

When she didn't say anything more, he added, "Well, I thought somehow you'd find it amusing, old Max from Notre Dame."

She stood. "No, Leon. They were a mighty hard bunch to laugh about."

He shrugged. "Well, keep Maurer on a righteous path. I worry when things look so smooth that there's something ugly floating under the surface."

She told Wayne about this at the Sam Hill. They didn't have their clothes off yet and she had almost called to cancel. But then time was growing short.

He listened to her with his brow creased. "Don't you think all we've done on the job is on the straight and narrow?"

She was quiet.

"Hey, now," he said. "You never cut me any special slack."

"I don't know, Wayne. What about surveying those barrow pits. I never had a contractor ask us to do that."

"I made them do it on every job Missouri let. Oklahoma, too."

She was frowning, recalling the chief's pink asphalt tickets, their blue perforated edges, blue bleeding into the pink like bruises on flesh.

Wayne shrugged. "Sandy, they pitched a fit about it up there, too." He reached and put a hand on her shoulder. "And they surveyed them anyhow. Listen, there's nothing out of the ordinary between us on the job."

She leaned forward to put her head in her hands, leaned just enough that he couldn't touch her shoulder and his fingertips ran down her back as his hand slipped. "I don't know, Wayne. The Ozarks is a tiny place. Contractors are a pretty tight bunch."

He turned away from her and sat on the edge of the bed facing the battered doorway and the twilight it leaked. It was getting dark earlier. Beneath her thighs she could feel him gripping the mattress. He would and he should, she thought, leave her right now, for her own good, for their own two goods. That's the kind of man she had come to love. And there it was—she loved him. Shit. Outside a car hissed along and its lights swept the room and threw her and Wayne's hunched shadows on the bare walls for an instant.

"I don't want to end this now," he said, his voice so soft she almost missed it. "But you're telling me this. What do you want to do?"

She stayed.

Driving the frontage road, checking the fencing, she stopped and inspected the guardrail Maurer had placed at the end of the deadly cul-de-sac. It was impressive—four big, thick steel warning bars covered in yellow, reflective vinyl, a red stop sign bordered with silver metallic paint and set off with iridescent orange medallions in rows. She rifled through the back of the spec book and found that the barrier met and exceeded any signage that might be called for.

Down the Yarberry's driveway she heard a car door slam. In the drive was a rusty Honda pickup truck with a U-Haul trailer hitched to it. Sandy popped the rolled spec book against her thigh a couple of times, then followed the drive down to the Yarberry's A-frame.

Mrs. Yarberry, Michelle, Sandy recalled from the police report and inquest, came from the house with a laundry basket full of quilts. Staggering, she managed to kick the door to the A-frame shut. Then she turned and stopped. Her face fell when she saw Sandy.

Mrs. Yarberry had cut her hair short, and the skin along her cheeks was the color of unpainted drywall. Near her cheekbone and down toward her right ear, scar tissue shined. No casts on her arms, so maybe they were never broken. "Ms. Coker," she said.

They stared at one another until Sandy looked away. On top of the folded quilts was a clock radio and a doll in overalls with a hardhat on its head.

"Will you open that truck for me?" Mrs. Yarberry asked.

Sandy opened the creaking door and stood back. When Mrs. Yarberry pushed the basket over the seat, the basket caught and bumped. The doll popped out and fell face down in the dirt. Mrs. Yarberry stared at it.

Finally Sandy bent and picked the doll up. Below the yellow hardhat it had a grin painted in black on its pale face, square, black painted eyes, and no nose. One of its plastic hands was open, and the other was shaped to hold things, a miniature hammer or wrench maybe, but there was nothing on his tool belt or tucked in the pockets of his overalls except a real copper blasting cap, its three wires bent like crazy metallic hairs. His overalls were smudged with food stains and his bottom and knees powdered red with dirt.

Sandy was about to hand her the doll when she caught Mrs. Yarberry's look, her cried-out, red-rimmed eyes.

"That was hers." Her swallow went terribly slow down her thin neck. "Said it was Daddy. Only toy I ever got her to play with. She about wore it bare loving it."

Without thinking, Sandy now clutched the doll to her chest. "Moving? You two are moving?"

"I am," Mrs. Yarberry said, glancing at the closed door to the A-frame. "I can't take this hell no more. He left me home with her and that goddamn wolf-dog and now I'm just alone all the time. I keep listening for her running like she would. But she never does come."

Sandy looked away for a moment. The hills that had always been a comfort seemed a purple wall, as if she were seeing them looming and closing like Mrs. Yarberry must have in her loneliness. "Is there anything I can do for you? Anything at all?"

Mrs. Yarberry glanced around the yard as if something that needed doing might pop up from the chert and red clay and pasture grass. "Is there anything?" Mrs. Yarberry asked, her voice the mutter of someone who had talked to herself for so long now, she did so even when company was present.

Mrs. Yarberry stared vacantly at Sandy, then fixed her eyes on the doll. "Keep that, will you? Maybe I got what I need."

SANDY AND WAYNE

Sandy set the little man on the kitchen counter in her double-wide. She could close her eyes and see the child flip and hear her French. Leaving the jobsite late on Fridays when Wayne had gone to Sedalia, she remembered seeing the lights on down in the A-frame, knowing those two, the mother and her baby girl, were safe and waiting for Daddy to come home from the tunnel through the mountain, waiting for when they could all be together.

The hollow of the doll's cupped fist began to trouble her. It wanted for a tool, for something to be ready for work. From his overalls, she pulled out the blasting cap, a magical souvenir the girl's daddy had brought home from the job. Down in the copper nubbin of the cap, Sandy saw it was still full of the ash blue, packed explosive. So much danger that little one had faced. So much carelessness. So much taken for granted. And in the end it got her. No wonder Mrs. Yarberry couldn't stay alone chewing on that surety.

Sandy pushed the blasting cap down in the

doll's cupped hand, a perfect fit. Now his smile meant something. He was ready for work again.

There was a knock. She let Wayne in. He was giddy and reached out to hug her, but stopped himself.

"Hey, now," he said, kneading her shoulders but holding her at arm's length.

She patted one of his hands and sat down again on the stool by the counter. He took the bar seat, the one with a Naugahyde back that her dad used to sit in.

When she was quiet too long, he picked up the doll. "Who's this happy fellow?"

She was crying silently and trying to hide it facing away from him. "He belonged to that poor baby girl. The Yarberry kid."

Wayne set him down carefully. "How'd you come by him?"

"She was packing. Mother was. She's leaving him. It was too much for her."

"She left poor Bob the Builder behind?"

Sandy shook her head, furious and wet with

her tears now, which she raked aside with the heel of her hand. "She wanted me to have him. Said she had enough."

Wayne waited a long time in silence, and the shadows lengthened. She wanted him to comfort her and at the same time it was the last thing she wanted, to be reminded that he was good and caring, and, even worse, he understood her. And she could tell he was reading that; he knew she was conflicted. It made the pit of her stomach burn.

"This little fellow's sure enough seen adventures," he said softly. She could hear the canvas of the doll's overalls scooting along the countertop. "He was loved a lot, no doubt."

"Goddamn it, Wayne."

He hushed, and she longed for him to get angry and make an exit. But he waited once more, and she could almost feel his strong shoulders slumping. A weight was on the two of them, her and Wayne, dark, thick, and as unstoppable as nightfall.

"Listen, the specs are published on that next

job," Wayne said. "We're about to marshal out. We'll get the bid."

She turned to him, and his look was anything but confident. He looked crushed, and that was exactly how she thought he would look. "Wayne, why'd any of this have to happen? That poor kid? Me and you?"

"That old man," he added, as if he were wondering, too, and going back to the start. "Would you rather it had not? At least, me and you, I mean?"

"I don't know. Right now, Wayne, I just don't know."

With care, he set the doll back where Sandy had it, but fiddled with the hardhat until it set rakishly. The happy doll's expression was transformed, yet Sandy couldn't tell if it now looked as if the thing had been walloped and knocked silly, or as if it had somehow realized it was about to be set loose and fancy free.

"Listen, maybe I better go," Wayne said, standing up. "Maybe tonight just ain't our night."

"Maybe," she agreed. But she held her hand

out to him, and he caught it fast, rubbed her fingertips with his thumb. "You'll let me know what happens on the bid?"

He nodded.

When the door shut, she waited a long time alone in the dark before going to the horses.

The time came for muster out, one of the final meetings between the lead inspector and the contractor's foremen. Sandy needed to cover the status of the job's remaining payouts, any construction items in dispute, and deliver the short laundry list of final tasks to be completed before Maurer could marshal forces and move on. Completion of the list meant a happy parting, though she had seen contractors leave without meeting the muster list and then head straight for court. Or like Rust, dissolve and leave rutted, unfinished lanes, mazes of ragged excavations, and miasmas of silt. Maurer had whipped the job into shape in just over eighteen months. They were about to make a killing. They didn't have to start from scratch, and Rust, in its own blundering way, had finished some of the heaviest lifting for them.

She and Wayne had taken a cooling off and he had spent some time back in Sedalia, much of his work being finished on AR 4005. When they were back together, she felt things strangely refreshed. They both did all they could to avoid the topic of what was to be done. They drank harder, rode longer, and made love roughly and resolutely, as if good sex were a cavaletti one could set higher and higher. Yet, watching his taillights vanish Sunday evenings, she felt even more empty and arid. It was as if in all their efforts to make it seem like their loving meant something, it meant less than ever before.

She brought the carryall to a stop in the gravel lot. Slowly she removed the muster out list from her clipboard and made sure she had the extra copies.

It was the first cool morning in a long time. There in front of the Maurer trailer gathered around a pearl white Lincoln Continental were the five main foremen, among them Wayne, Chris with the bridges, Andy the lead foreman, and Old Man Maurer. She had the windows rolled up and the heater on, so she turned the carryall off and watched them. Mr. Maurer was making a speech it seemed, and the five of them were listening with reverence. There was a quart bottle of Budweiser and a stack of Styrofoam cups on the hood of the Lincoln. Sandy had never seen any contractor do anything such as this, not at nine in the morning, and she wouldn't deign to join the circle even if she knew what it meant. After Maurer said some more, Wayne handed each foreman a cup, and last, one for Maurer, who then poured beer for everyone. They were quiet.

Old Man Maurer raised his cup and shouted something like a motto in what sounded like a foreign language. The men all raised their cups and answered back, another foreign phrase.

At first she stifled a laugh—this was silly. What were they, Shriners? Elks with secret handshakes?

But then as she watched Wayne with them, watched them all laughing and toasting and clasping one another's arms, pounding one another's backs, she stilled. They were conquerors, like an army that had just brought low the last enemy castle. Even Andy, the lead foreman, held Wayne's handshake a long while and looked him warmly in the eyes. Old Man Maurer joined Andy and clasped Wayne's shoulder. Wayne raised his cup, shouted the foreign words again, and they answered. They were brothers in arms. That's what Wayne had with them. That was what she was wanting him to leave.

After a good dinner near the Sam Hill, they spent that evening together sitting on her couch with their clothes on, and the television flickering but low.

"That was some ceremony you all had this morning," she said.

Wayne smiled. "Old Man Maurer taught us

all a lot. Those are his five, you know. Not one man in the bunch been with him less than twenty years."

"Damn." It was impressive. On the contractor's end, the business was vagabond in the extreme. Beyond the highest paid managers, foremen didn't often stay with a roving contractor such as Maurer for long. "So what was that you all were yelling?" She asked it carefully, knowing how men did not care to be belittled about manly things.

Wayne smiled. "Maurers are German. But it's something he picked up flying against Germans." He raised an imaginary glass. "*Per ardua ad aspera*."

She slouched, leaning her back against his side. "What's it mean?" She felt him laugh. "You all don't know what it means?" she asked.

"Not perfectly. I mean, it's Latin. Not my best subject."

She tilted her head back to look at his eyes, then found herself laughing, too. "Like you couldn't tell me it means any old thing, Wayne. Jesus, I don't know any Latin."

He patted her hip. "It means sort of 'In hardship to the stars.' At least that's what I always told myself it meant."

She watched the television strobe and warp her trailer walls and the kitchen cabinets. He stroked the back of her hair, and she found her lips trying to say the Latin. A siren on TV bothered her concentration. "What do you all say back?" When she tilted her head again to catch his eyes, she was stricken to see he was not watching the television, but watching her, and his eyes were wet at their edges.

"Oh that's German. '*Erobern.*' That one I know for sure. It means, 'We conquer!' "

She took his arm and held it against her, pleased but frightened by how very good it felt to sit with this man and talk. "And you all say that at the end of every job?"

Wayne nodded and kissed the top of her head. "Twenty years."

She did not hear him leave, but woke on the couch alone when the television flashed and the national anthem played, and troops planted the flag on some terrible-looking island far away.

DAILY DIARY: AR4005 GREENLAND TO WEST FORK—COKER, AHTD

Working conditions: Good for all phases of construction.

Contractor able to employ 60% of all normal forces and equipment.

Engineering activities: None.

Contractor's Work—Roadway: Painting and striping 460+00 to 5460+99 Sta.

Contractor's Work—Structures: Br. 4581A Sandblasting finger joint at bent #9.

Visitors and decisions: None.

Instructions to Contractor: None (Job is substantially complete).

Wayne knocked and ducked under the doorway, took his hat off. She realized just then everywhere they went together, whenever he set foot in a building, he removed his hat. Here all along she had taken that for granted.

"That was real impressive," she said. "Those semis arriving at just the minute when you were moving the last yard." There was no way around it—Maurer was a solid company, ruthless and efficient as a Roman legion.

When he didn't grin, she felt an ache start in her abdomen and it was soon running down her groin. After today all their forces would be long gone. He had to go.

"We didn't get that bid south of the tunnel." He ran his tongue over his lips.

"Back to Missouri, then?"

He nodded. "Up on the Jack's Fork and Eleven Point. Real pretty country."

Outside some temp who just got paid his bonus at the job's end was whooping and honking.

Gravel spattered under his truck leaving in a hurry. He would be dead drunk in a couple more hours and looking for work again by next week.

"Sandy, why don't you come on up there with me?"

She shook her head.

He swallowed hard, and for once looked stunned and at a loss, his blue eyes hovering on a spot above her head. When he got hold of himself he said, "You know, one time you said you needed someone you could count on. From what I seen of you, you don't need anybody, Sandy Coker."

She was sure it was more than he wanted to say, more than the dusty old AHTD trailer could hold, it seemed.

"I really hope you're right."

"That's why I want you up there with me."

"I can't," she said. "I just can't, Wayne. You know what I got here."

They couldn't bear to look at one another for a long while.

"Well, listen, it's not like I don't know how to

drive from Sedalia to here." He paused, watching her closely. "I can come on weekends. If you'll have me."

She was very still. "I've lived that way before. It doesn't work. That's not . . . I'm not young enough to believe in weekend love anymore." She couldn't help but think of Mrs. Yarberry and all that time alone and no help when disaster came. And it would come.

He looked at her, his jaw thrust forward. "So is that all we boil down to, Sandy? A little land, some horses, a retirement coming?"

"A big salary? A good crew? Twenty years?" she threw back. She bowed her head, sorry that she had said it all so sharply. When she looked up at him, his eyes were fastened on a patch of nothing in the linoleum in front of his boot tips. His jaw rippled. "Wayne, why are you doing this to us? You need to go. Why talk?"

He looked up slowly, and where she expected him to harden his gaze and turn from her, his eyes widened as if he were just realizing something. "I guess I thought maybe we . . . that together we were changing ourselves into something better, Sandy, you and me."

It took a great effort to keep the pain from cracking her voice. "Well, I guess we're not, Wayne." From outside the small window, the brown and red of turned leaves made the air in the trailer seem afire. And yet it was cool, late autumn. It was going to kill her if she had to tell him to leave.

Finally he stirred and said, "Well, listen, if you're ever up there, we shouldn't be hard to find. We'll be on some highway."

She tried hard to shut out the sound of his feet creaking on the metal steps, and finally the crunch of the Camaro's door closing. He never would get that car re-primered and painted. He would drive it around half-finished until at last he had to let it go.

On the ridge, Trick of Light stopped walking, and Sandy awakened from the quilt of numbness she was piecing around herself. Even if her breeding was diluted, Trick was still a thoroughbred and in every blood vessel there ran the possibility of meanness or inexplicable fright. But the horse remained steady beneath her and let loose a long, sputtering snort, almost as if content with the view. The filly had tired of walking without direction and simply decided to stop where the light suited her.

It was the last of the gloaming. Venus and the moon struck the circumference of advancing night with a frail silver. Fall had come and gone. When? She made her living out of doors and knew intimately every increment of change in nature. For the first time since she was a girl, a season had stolen up on her. The silver light on the dew promised frost by next week.

Where had the comet gone? Why had she not seen it fading? Had it faded or just vanished? The night sky bore no trace of it no matter how hard she stared.

But reason said it had to be out there, careening along, unobserved, a streak that no one she knew would ever have sight of again. She recalled something she had caught on the radio about its lonely, vast circuit. This was its one season over the Ozarks.

Somewhere out there now on the highways they had made together, he was moving on, though she could not see him, might never see him around here again, driving that gray Camaro, a wedge of fog flying through the night, accelerating, dwindling, gone; but somehow in her thoughts, he remained, like a hard crust of ice and light tearing an earthly arc from her hills and Greenland to faraway Sedalia.

She ran her fingers through Trick's coarse mane and pushed her hand up the filly's powerful neck. "Oh, Trick," she whispered.

It was then that they both heard tires breaching the cattle guard and coming on over the barrier. And the filly, without any urging, flicked its ears, then bore Sandy up the hill to be with him.

ACKNOWLEDGMENTS

My thanks to Miller Williams, who gave me my first job in publishing, for significantly instructing me, "There may be no higher calling than writing a good country music song."

My thanks to Randolph Thomas, best friend through all these years, for reading this work.

My deep thanks to Heather Jacobs, the best fiction editor I may ever have the luck to work with, for nurturing every line of this.

My astonished thanks to Dane Bahr, for making beautiful books of fiction happen.

My thanks to all those on the Arkansas Highway

and Transportation Department for trusting me for three sweltering summers, for allowing me a seat in many dusty carryalls, and for tolerating, every lunch hour and transit, the spectacle of a surveyor writing longhand in a ring-bound notebook and hardly socializing. "Writin' his memoirs!" as High Rod Harold so kindly defended me.

And unending, boundless thanks to my wife, Tammy Gebhart Yates, for believing always in me, even when I did not.

PHOTO: ELLIE BANKS

Born and reared in Springfield, Missouri, Steve Yates is an M.F.A. graduate from the creative writing program at the University of Arkansas. He is the winner of the Juniper Prize in Fiction and in April 2013, University of Massachusetts Press published his collection *Some Kinds of Love: Stories.* He is assistant director/marketing director at University Press of Mississippi in Jackson, and lives in Flowood with his wife, Tammy.

CPSIA information can be obtained
at www.ICGtesting.com
Printed in the USA
LVHW022122051120
670845LV00014B/1801